D1093648

When I'm the
Mommy

When I'm the Mommy

By Andrea & Margaret Tee

This is a work of fiction. Any resemblance to persons living or dead should be plainly apparent to them and those who know them, especially if the author has been kind enough to have provided their real names. All events described herein may or may not have actually happened.

First edition March 2023

ISBN 979-8-218-17459-0 (hardcover)
ISBN 979-8-218-17460-6 (ebook)

This book is dedicated to
Stephen Tee Sr.

*Thanks for being
the "Mommy"*

"When I'm the Mommy," said Gwendolyn to her Teddy, "I'm going to be nicer than my mommy. I'm going to let my little girl do

whatever she wants!"

Teddy didn't think so,
but he didn't say anything.

"When I'm the Mommy," said Gwendolyn, "I'm going to let my little girl get a new pet, *anytime she wants.*"

Teddy didn't think so,
but he didn't say anything.

"When I'm the Mommy," said Gwendolyn, "I'm going to let my little girl stay up as late as she wants,

even for midnight cartoons."

Teddy didn't think so,
but he didn't say anything.

"When I'm the Mommy," said Gwendolyn, "I'm going to let my little girl eat anything she wants,

even candy for breakfast."

Teddy didn't think so,
but he didn't say anything.

"When I'm the Mommy," said Gwendolyn, "I'm going to buy my little girl **every toy she wants.**"

TOYS
CLOSED

Teddy didn't think so,
but he didn't say anything.

"There is one thing that Mommy does do just right," said Gwendolyn to her Teddy. "When I'm the mommy, I'm going to give my little girl **lots of hugs...** just like she does."

Teddy *did* **think so!**
He still didn't say anything,
but Teddy smiled.

Gwendolyn

Gwendolyn is the granddaughter of the original author and illustrator, on the maternal side.

She is the niece of the illustrator of this version of the story.

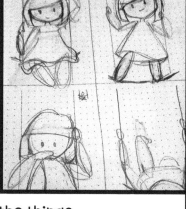

Gwendolyn is about 2 years old in the picture to the right. She served as the inspiration for the update of this story.

She would absolutely say all of the things in this book.

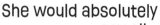

"Teddy"

According to Gwendolyn's mother, "Teddy" is a stuffed dog and Gwendolyn's favorite stuffed animal. "Teddy" previously belonged to Gwendolyn's father as a child.

The original story, written and illustrated by Margaret Tee, is included on the following pages and some of the original artwork was adapted directly for this version.

Margaret passed suddenly in 1999 and left behind four children and a husband.

Her book was never published. The original text and illustrations are included on the next few pages. I hope this story inspires you to cherish and share your own family's art.

when I'm the
Mommy

Original Story and Illustrations
by Margaret "Peggy" Tee

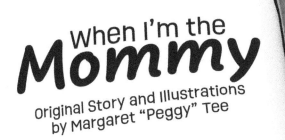

"When I'm the mommy" said Susan to her teddy, "I'm going to be nicer than my mommy." "I'm going to let my little girl do whatever she wants. Teddy didn't think so, but he didn't say anything.

When I'm the mommy said Susan, I'm going to let my little girl get a new pet, any time she wants.

Teddy didn't think so, but he didn't say anything.

When I'm the mommy said Susan, I'm going to let my little girl stay up as long as she wants, even for the late, late, show

Teddy didn't think so, but he didn't say anything.

When I'm the mommy said Susan, I'm going to let my little girl eat anything she wants, even M&M's for breakfast

Teddy didn't think so, but he didn't say anything.

When I'm the mommy said Susan, I'm going to buy my little girl every-thing she wants

Teddy didn't think so, but he didn't say anything

There is one thing that mommy does do just right, said Susan to Teddy. When I'm the mommy, I'm going to give my little girl lots of hugs, just like she does. Teddy _did_ think so, and he still didn't say anything, but Teddy smiled.

The
End

Color Me!

CPSIA information can be obtained
at www.ICGtesting.com
Printed in the USA
JSHW051227140423
40318JS00002B/15

9 798218 174590